This book belongs to:

....

Published by Award Publications Limited,
The Old Riding School, The Welbeck Estate,
Worksop, Nottinghamshire, S80 3LR

www.awardpublications.co.uk

10 3

Printed in Malaysia

Award Young Readers

Old Macdonald on His Farm

Rewritten by Jackie Andrews

Illustrated by John Bennett

AWARD PUBLICATIONS LIMITED

Old Macdonald had a farm, E-I-E-I-O!

And on that farm he had some cows, E-I-E-I-O!

With a moo-moo here, a moo-moo there,
Here a moo, there a moo, everywhere a
moo-moo.

Old Macdonald had a farm, E-I-E-I-O!

Old Macdonald had a farm, E-I-E-I-O!
And on that farm he had some sheep,
E-I-E-I-O!

With a baa-baa here, a baa-baa there,
Here a baa, there a baa, everywhere a baa-baa.

A moo-moo here, a moo-moo there,
Here a moo, there a moo, everywhere
a moo-moo.

Old Macdonald had a farm, E-I-E-I-O!

Old Macdonald had a farm, E-I-E-I-O!
And on that farm he had some pigs,
E-I-E-I-O!

With an oink-oink here, an oink-oink there,
Here an oink, there an oink, everywhere
an oink-oink.

A baa-baa here, a baa-baa there,
Here a baa, there a baa, everywhere
   a baa-baa.
A moo-moo here, a moo-moo there,
Here a moo, there a moo, everywhere
   a moo-moo.

Old Macdonald had a farm, E-I-E-I-O!

Old Macdonald had a farm, E-I-E-I-O!
And on that farm he had some ducks,
    E-I-E-I-O!

With a quack-quack here, a quack-quack there,
Here a quack, there a quack, everywhere
    a quack-quack.

An oink-oink here, an oink-oink there,
Here an oink, there an oink, everywhere
   an oink-oink,
A baa-baa here, a baa-baa there,
Here a baa, there a baa, everywhere a baa-baa.

A moo-moo here, a moo-moo there,
Here a moo, there a moo, everywhere
 a moo-moo.
Old Macdonald had a farm, E-I-E-I-O!

Old Macdonald had a farm, E-I-E-I-O!
And on that farm he had some hens, E-I-E-I-O!

With a cluck-cluck here, a cluck-cluck there,
Here a cluck, there a cluck, everywhere
   a cluck-cluck.

A quack-quack here, a quack-quack there,
Here a quack, there a quack, everywhere
　　a quack-quack.
An oink-oink here, an oink-oink there,
Here an oink, there an oink, everywhere
　　an oink-oink.

A baa-baa here, a baa-baa there,
Here a baa, there a baa, everywhere
   a baa-baa.
A moo-moo here, a moo-moo there,
Here a moo, there a moo, everywhere
   a moo-moo.

Old Macdonald had a farm, E-I-E-I-O!

Old Macdonald had a farm, E-I-E-I-O!
And on that farm he had some dogs, E-I-E-I-O!

With a woof-woof here, a woof-woof there,
Here a woof, there a woof, everywhere
a woof-woof.

A cluck-cluck here, a cluck-cluck there,
Here a cluck, there a cluck, everywhere
 a cluck-cluck.
A quack-quack here, a quack-quack there,
Here a quack, there a quack, everywhere
 a quack-quack.
An oink-oink here, an oink-oink there,
Here an oink, there an oink, everywhere
 an oink-oink.

A baa-baa here, a baa-baa there,
Here a baa, there a baa, everywhere
   a baa-baa.
And a moo-moo here, a moo-moo there,
Here a moo, there a moo, everywhere
   a moo-moo.
Old Macdonald had a farm, E-I-E-I-O!